"In a cellar"

By

Harriet Prescott Spofford

British Library Cataloguing-in-Publication Data
A catalogue record for this book is available from the
British Library

Harriet Elizabeth Prescott Spofford

Harriet Elizabeth Prescott Spofford was born on 3rd April 1835 in Calais, Maine, United States. She is now best known for her novels, poems and detective stories – a true pioneer of the American detective genre. When she was still a baby, Spofford's parents moved to Newburyport, Massachusetts, where she chose to stay for almost her entire life. Although she spent many of her winters in Boston and Washington D.C., Newburyport remained always close to Spofford's heart.

She attended the Putnam Free School in Newburyport and Pinkerton Academy in Derry, New Hampshire from 1853 to 1855. At Newburyport her prize essay on Hamlet drew the attention of Thomas Wentworth Higginson (a Unitarian minister, author, abolitionist, and soldier), who soon became her friend and gave Spofford much needed counsel and encouragement throughout her career. When Spofford was in her mid-twenties, her parents suffered from ill health, and of necessity she was set to work as a writer, sometimes labouring fifteen hours a day. She contributed to various Boston story papers for small fees, but her first major success came in 1859; this was Spofford's submission to *Atlantic Monthly* (a literary and cultural magazine) of a story about Parisian life, 'In a Cellar'. The magazine's editor, James Russell Lowell, first believed the story to be a translation and withheld it from publication. Reassured it was original, he eventually published it, and the narrative established her reputation. After this success, Spofford became a welcome contributor to the chief periodicals of the United States, both of prose and poetry.

Spofford's fiction had very little in common with what was regarded as representative of 'the New England mind.' Her **gothic romances** were set apart by luxuriant descriptions and an unconventional handling of female **stereotypes** of the day. Her writing was ideal and intense in feeling, revelling in sensuous delights and material splendour. Nowhere was this more evident than, in 'Circumstance', an allegorical short story which takes place in the woods of Maine. In this tale, the protagonist comes into contact with the Indian Devil, forcing her to come to terms with her own life, sexuality and fears. By the end of the story, her husband shoots the Devil with his shotgun in one hand and their baby in the other while the **'true Indian Devils'** destroy their home and town. When Wentworth Higginson asked Emily Dickinson whether she had read Spofford's work, Dickinson replied, 'I read Miss Prescott's 'Circumstance,' but it followed me in the dark, so I avoided her.' Other notable works include *The Thief in the Night* (1872), *The Servant Girl Question* (1881), *A Scarlet Poppy and Other Stories* (1894), and *The Fairy Changeling* (1910).

In 1865, at the age of thirty, the authoress married Richard S. Spofford, a Boston lawyer, and the couple resided on Deer Island overlooking the **Merrimack River** at **Amesbury**, a suburb of Newburyport. They lived here for the rest of their lives. Harriet Prescott Spofford died on 14th August 1921, aged eighty-six.

In a cellar

IT WAS THE DAY of Madame de St. Cyr's dinner, an event I never missed; for, the mistress of a mansion in the Faubourg St. Germain, there still lingered about her the exquisite grace and good-breeding peculiar to the old regime, that insensibly communicates itself to the guests till they move in an atmosphere of ease that constitutes the charm of home. One was always sure of meeting desirable and well-assorted people here, and a contre-temps was impossible. Moreover, the house was not at the command of all; and Madame de St. Cyr, with the daring strength which, when found in a woman at all, should, to be endurable, be combined with a sweet but firm restraint, rode rough-shod over the parvenus of the Empire, and was resolute enough to insulate herself even among the old noblesse, who, as all the world knows, insulate themselves from the rest of France. There were rare qualities in this woman, and were I to have selected one who with an even hand should carry a snuffy candle through a magazine of powder, my choice would have devolved upon her; and she would have done it.

I often looked, and not unsuccessfully, to discern what heritage her daughter had in these little affairs. Indeed, to one like myself, Delphine presented the worthier study. She wanted the airy charm of manner, the suavity and tenderness of her mother, — a deficiency easily to be pardoned in one of such delicate and extraordinary beauty. And perhaps her face was the truest index of her mind; not that it ever transparently displayed a genuine emotion, — Delphine was too well bred for that, — but the outline of her features had a keen regular precision, as if cut in a gem. Her exquisite color seldom varied, her eyes were like blue steel, she was statuelike and stony. But had one paused there, pronouncing her hard and impassive, he had committed an error. She had no great capability for passion, but she was not to be deceived; one metallic flash of her eye would cut like a sword through the whole mesh of entanglements with which you had surrounded her; and frequently, when alone with her, you perceived cool recesses in her nature, sparkling and pleasant, which jealously guarded themselves from a nearer approach. She was infinitely spirituelle; compared to her, Madame herself was heavy.

At the first, I had seen that Delphine must be the wife of a diplomate. What diplomate? For a time asking myself the question seriously, I decided in the negative, which did not, however, prevent Delphine from fulfilling her destiny, since there were others. She was, after all, like a draught of rich old wine, all fire and sweetness. These things were not generally seen in her; I was more favored than many; and I looked at her with pitiless perspicacious eyes. Nevertheless, I had not the least advantage; it was, in fact, between us, diamond cut diamond, — which, oddly enough, brings me back to my story.

Some years previously, I had been sent on a special mission to the government at Paris, and having finally executed it, I resigned the post, and resolved to make my residence there, since it is the only place on earth where one can live. Every morning I half expect to see the country, beyond the city, white with an encampment of the nations, who, having peacefully flocked there over night, wait till the Rue St. Honoré shall run out and greet them. It surprises me, sometimes, that those pretending to civilization are content to remain at a distance. What experience have they of life, — not to mention gayety and pleasure, but of the great purpose of life, — society? Man evidently is gregarious; Fourier's fables are founded on fact; we are nothing without our opposites, our fellows, our lights and shadows, colors, relations, combinations, our point d'appui, and our angle of sight. An isolated man is immensurable; he is also unpicturesque, unnatural, untrue. He is no longer the lord of Nature, animal and vegetable, — but Nature is the lord of him; the trees, skies, flowers, predominate, and he is in as bad taste as green and blue, or as an oyster in a vase of roses. The race swings naturally to clusters. It being admitted, then, that society is our normal state, where is it to be obtained in such perfection as at Paris? Show me the urbanity, the generosity in trifles, better than sacrifice, the incuriousness and freedom, the grace, and wit, and honor, that will equal such as I find here. Morality, — we were not speaking of it, — the intrusion is unnecessary; must that word with Anglo-Saxon pertinacity dog us round the world? A hollow mask, which Vice now and then lifts for a breath of air, I grant you this state may be called; but since I find the vice elsewhere, countenance my preference for the accompanying mask. But even this is vanishing; such drawing-rooms as Mme. de St. Cyr's are less and less frequent. Yet, though the delightful spell of the last century daily dissipates itself, and we are not now what we were twenty years ago, still Paris is, and will be to the end of time, for a cosmopolitan, the pivot on which the world revolves.

It was, then, as I have said, the day of Mme. de St. Cyr's dinner. Punctually at the hour, I presented myself, — for I have always esteemed it the least courtesy which a guest can render, that he should not cool his hostess's dinner.

The usual choice company waited. There was the Marquis of G., the ambassador from home; Col. Leigh, an attaché of that embassy; the Spanish and Belgian ministers; — all of whom, with myself, completed a diplomatic circle. There were also wits and artists, but no ladies whose beauty exceeded that of the St. Cyrs. With nearly all of this assemblage I held certain relations, so that I was immediately at ease. G. was the only one whom, perhaps, I would rather not have met, although we were the best of friends. They awaited but one, the Baron Stahl. Meanwhile Delphine stood coolly taking the measurement of the Marquis of G., while her mother entertained one and another guest with a low-toned flattery, gentle interest, or lively narration, as the case might demand.

In a country where a coup d'état was as easily given as a box on the ear, we all attentively watched for the arrival of one who had been sent from a neighboring empire to negotiate a loan for the tottering throne of this. Nor was expectation kept long on guard. In a moment, "His Excellency, the Baron Stahl!" was announced.

The exaggeration of his low bow to Mme. de St. Cyr, the gleam askance of his black eye, the absurd simplicity of his dress, did not particularly please me. A low forehead, straight black brows, a beardless cheek with a fine color which give him a fictitiously youthful appearance, were the most striking traits of his face; his person was not to be found fault with; but he boldly evinced his admiration for Delphine, and with a wicked eye.

As we were introduced, he assured me, in pure English, that he had pleasure in making the acquaintance of a gentleman whose services were so distinguished.

I, in turn, assured him of my pleasure in meeting a gentleman who appreciated them.

I had arrived at the house of Mme. de St. Cyr with a load on my mind, which for four weeks had weighed there; but before I thus spoke, it was lifted and gone. I had seen the Baron Stahl before, although not previously aware of it; and now, as he bowed, talked my native tongue so smoothly, drew a glove over the handsome hand upon whose first finger shone the only incongruity of his attire, a broad gold ring, holding a gaudy red stone, — as he stood smiling and expectant before me, a sudden chain of events flashed through my mind, an instantaneous heat, like lightning, welded them into logic. A great problem was resolved. For a second, the breath seemed snatched from my lips; the next, a lighter, freer man never trod in diplomatic shoes.

I really beg your pardon, — but perhaps from long usage, it has become impossible for me to tell a straight story. It is absolutely necessary to inform you of events already transpired.

In the first place, then, I, at this time, possessed a valet, the pink of valets, an Englishman, — and not the less valuable to me in a foreign capital, that, notwithstanding his long residence, he was utterly unable to speak one word of French intelligibly. Reading and writing it readily, his thick tongue could master scarcely a syllable. The adroitness and perfection with which he performed the duties of his place were unsurpassable. To a certain extent I was obliged to admit him into my confidence; I was not at all in his. In dexterity and despatch he equalled the advertisements. He never condescended to don my cast-off apparel, but, disposing of it, always arrayed himself in plain but gentlemanly garments. These do not complete the list of Hay's capabilities. He speculated. Respectable tenements in London called him landlord; in the funds certain sums lay subject to his order; to a profitable farm in Hants he contemplated future retirement; and passing upon the Bourse, I have received a grave bow, and have left him in conversation with an eminent capitalist respecting consols, drafts, exchange, and other erudite mysteries, where I yet find myself in the A B C. Thus not only was my valet a free-born Briton, but a landed proprietor. If the Rothschilds blacked your boots or shaved your chin, your emotions might be akin to mine. When this man, who had an interest in the India traders, brought the hot water into my dressing-room, of a morning, the Antipodes were tributary to me. To what extent might any little irascibility of mine drive a depression in the market! and I knew, as he brushed my hat, whether stocks rose or fell. In one respect, I was essentially like our Saxon ancestors, — my servant was a villain. If I had been merely a civilian, in any purely private capacity, having leisure to attend to personal concerns in the midst of the delicate specialties intrusted to me from the cabinet at home, the possession of so inestimable a valet might have bullied me beyond endurance. As it was, I found it rather agreeable than otherwise. He was tacitly my secretary of finance.

Several years ago, a diamond of wonderful size and beauty, having wandered from the East, fell into certain imperial coffers among our Continental neighbors; and at the same time some extraordinary intelligence, essential to the existence, so to speak, of that government, reached a person there who fixed as its price this diamond. After a while he obtained it, but, judging that prudence lay in departure, took it to England, where it was purchased for an enormous sum by the Duke of — as he will remain an unknown quantity, let us say X. There are probably not a dozen such diamonds in the world, — certainly not three in England. It rejoiced in such flowery appellatives as the Sea of Splendor, the Moon of Milk; and, of course, those who had but parted with it under protest, as it were, determined to obtain it again at all hazards; — they were never famous for scrupulosity The Duke of X. was aware of this, and, for a time, the gem had lain idle, its glory muffled in a casket; but finally, on some grand occasion a few months prior to the period of which I have spoken above, it was determined to set it in the Duchess's coronet. Accordingly, one day, it was given by her son, the Marquis of G., into the hands of their solicitor, who should deliver it to her Grace's jeweller. It lay in a small shagreen case, and before the Marquis left, the solicitor placed the case in a flat leathern box, where lay a chain of most singular workmanship, the clasp of which was deranged. This chain was very broad, of a style known as the brickwork, but every brick was a tiny gem, set in a delicate filagree linked with the next, and the whole rainbowed lustrousness moving at your will, like the scales of some gorgeous Egyptian serpent; — the solicitor was to take this also to the jeweller. Having laid the box in his private desk, Ulster, his confidential clerk, locked it, while he bowed the Marquis down. Returning immediately, the solicitor took the flat box and drove to the jeweller's. He found the latter so crowded with customers, it being the fashionable hour, as to be unable to attend to him; he, however, took the solicitor into his inner room, a dark fire-proof place, and there quickly deposited the box within a safe, which stood inside another, like a Japanese puzzle, and the solicitor, seeing the doors double-locked and secured, departed; the other promising to attend to the matter on the morrow.

Early the next morning, the jeweller entered his dark room, and proceeded to unlock the safe. This being concluded, and the inner one also thrown open, he found the box in a last and entirely, as he had always believed, secret compartment. Anxious to see this wonder, this Eye of Morning, and Heart of Day, he eagerly loosened the band and unclosed the box. It was empty. There was no chain there; the diamond was missing. The sweat streamed from his forehead, his clothes were saturated, he believed himself the victim of a delusion. Calling an assistant, every article and nook in the dark room was examined. At last, in an extremity of despair, he sent for the solicitor, who arrived in a breath. The jeweller's alarm hardly equalled that of the other. In his sudden dismay, he at first forgot the circumstances and dates relating to the affair; afterward was doubtful. The Marquis of G. was summoned, the police called in, the jeweller given into custody. Every breath the solicitor continued to draw only built up his ruin. He swallowed laudanum, but, by making it an overdose, frustrated his own design. He was assured, on his recovery, that no suspicion attached to him. The jeweller now asseverated that the diamond had never been given to him; but though the jeweller had committed perjury, this was, nevertheless, strictly true. Of course, whoever had the stone would not attempt to dispose of it at present, and, though communications were opened with the general European police, there was very little to work upon. But by means of this last step the former possessors became aware of its loss, and I make no doubt had their agents abroad immediately.

Meanwhile, the case hung here, complicated and tantalizing, when one morning I woke in London. No sooner had G. heard of my arrival than he called, and, relating the affair, requested my assistance. I confess myself to have been interested, — foolishly so, I thought afterward; but we all have our weaknesses, and diamonds were mine. In company with the Marquis, I waited upon the solicitor, who entered into the few details minutely, calling frequently upon Ulster, a young, fresh-looking man, for corroboration. We then drove to the jeweller's new quarters, took him, under charge of the officers, to his place of business, where he nervously showed me every point that could bear upon the subject, and ended by exclaiming, that he was ruined, and all for a stone he had never seen. I sat quietly for a few moments. It stood, then, thus: — G. had given the thing to the solicitor, seen it put into the box, seen the box put into the desk; but while the confidential clerk, Ulster, locked the desk, the solicitor waited on the Marquis to the door, — returning, took the box, without opening it again, to the jeweller, who, in the hurry, shut it up in his safe, also without opening it. The case was perfectly clear. These mysterious things are always so simple! You know now as well as I, who took the diamond.

I did not choose to volunteer, but assented, on being desired. The police and I were old friends; they had so often assisted me, that I was not afraid to pay them in kind, and accordingly agreed to take charge of the case, still retaining their aid, should I require it. The jeweller was now restored to his occupation, although still subjected to a rigid surveillance, and I instituted inquiries into the recent movements of the young man Ulster. The case seemed to me to have been very blindly conducted. But, though all that was brought to light concerning him in London was perfectly fair and aboveboard, it was discovered that, not long since, he had visited Paris, — on the solicitor's business, of course, but gaining thereby an opportunity to transact any little affairs of his own. This was fortunate; for if any one could do anything in Paris, it was myself.

It is not often that I act as a detective. But one homogeneous to every situation could hardly play a pleasanter part for once. I have thought that our great masters in theory and practice, Machiavel and Talleyrand, were hardly more, on a large scale.

I was about to return to Paris, but resolved to call previously on the solicitor again. He welcomed me warmly, although my suspicions had not been imparted to him, and, with a more cheerful heart than had lately been habitual to him, entered into an animated conversation respecting the great case of Biter v. Bit, then absorbing so much of the public attention, frequently addressing Ulster, whose remarks were always pertinent, brief, and clear. As I sat actively discussing the topic, feeling no more interest in it than in the end of that cigar I just cut off, and noting exactly every look and motion of the unfortunate youth, I recollect the curious sentiment that filled me regarding him. What injury had he done me, that I should pursue him with punishment? Me? I am, and every individual is, integral with the commonwealth. It was the commonwealth he had injured. Yet, even then, why was I the one to administer justice? Why not continue with my coffee in the morning, my kings and cabinets and national chess at noon, my opera at night, and let the poor devil go? Why, but that justice is brought home to every member of society, — that naked duty requires no shirking of such responsibility, — that, had I failed here, the crime might, with reason, lie at my door and multiply, the criminal increase himself?

Very possibly you will not unite with me; but these little catechisms are, once in a while, indispensable, to vindicate one's course to one's self.

This Ulster was a handsome youth; — the rogues have generally all the good looks. There was nothing else remarkable about him but his quickness; he was perpetually on the alert; by constant activity, the rust was never allowed to collect on his faculties; his sharpness was distressing, — he appeared subject to a tense strain. Now his quill scratched over the paper unconcernedly, while he could join as easily in his master's conversation:

nothing seemed to preoccupy him, or he held a mind open at every point. It is pitiful to remember him that morning, sitting quiet, unconscious, and free, utterly in the hands of that mighty Inquisition, the Metropolitan Police, with its countless arms, its cells and myrmidons in the remotest corners of the Continent, — at the mercy of so merciless a monster, and momently closer involved, like some poor prey round which a spider spins its bewildering web. It was also curious to observe the sudden suspicion that darkened his face at some innocent remark, — the quick shrinking and intrenched retirement, the manifest sting and rancor, as I touched his wound with a swift flash of my slender weapon and sheathed it again, and, after the thrust, the espionage, and the relief at believing it accidental. He had many threads to gather up and hold; — little electric warnings along them must have been constantly shocking him. He did that part well enough; it was a mistake, to begin with; he needed prudence. At that time I owed this Ulster nothing; now, however, I owe him a grudge, for some of the most harassing hours of my life were occasioned me by him. But I shall not cherish enmity on that account. With so promising a beginning, he will graduate and take his degree from the loftiest altitude in his line. Hemp is a narcotic; let it bring me forgetfulness.

In Paris I found it not difficult to trace such a person, since he was both foreign and unaccustomed. It was ascertained that he had posted several letters. A person of his description had been seen to drop a letter, the superscription of which had been read by one who picked it up for him. This superscription was the address of the very person who was likely to be the agent of the former possessors of the diamond, and had attracted attention. After all, — you know the Secret Force, — it was not so impossible to imagine what this letter contained, despite of its cipher. Such a person also had been met among the Jews, and at certain shops whose reputation was not of the clearest. He had called once or twice on Mme. de St. Cyr, on business relative to a vineyard adjoining her chateau in the Gironde, which she had sold to a wine merchant of England. I found a zest in the affair, as I pursued it.

We were now fairly at sea, but before long I found we were likely to remain there; in fact, nothing of consequence eventuated. I began to regret having taken the affair from the hands in which I had found it, and one day, it being a gala or some insatiable saint's day, I was riding, perplexed with that and other matters, and paying small attention to the passing crowd. I was vexed and mortified, and had fully decided to throw up the whole, — on such hairs do things hang, — when, suddenly turning a corner, my bridle-reins became entangled in the snaffle of another rider. I loosened them abstractedly, and not till it was necessary to bow to my strange antagonist on parting, did I glance up. The person before me was evidently not accustomed to play the dandy; he wore his clothes ill, sat his horse worse, and was uneasy in the saddle. The unmistakable air of the gamin was apparent beneath the superficies of the gentleman. Conspicuous on his costume, and wound like an order of merit upon his breast, glittered a chain, the chain, — each tiny brick-like gem spiked with a hundred sparks, and building a fabric of sturdy probabilities with the celerity of the genii in constructing Aladdin's palace. There, a cable to haul up the treasure, was the chain; — where was the diamond? I need not tell you how I followed this young friend, with what assiduity I kept him in sight, up and down, all day long, till, weary at last of his fine sport, as I certainly was of mine, he left his steed in stall and fared on his way a-foot. Still pursuing, now I threaded quay and square, street and alley, till he disappeared in a small shop, in one of those dark crowded lanes leading eastward from the Pont Neuf, in the city. It was the sign of a marchand des armures, and having provided myself with those persuasive arguments, a sergent-de-ville and a gendarme, I entered.

A place more characteristic it would be impossible to find. Here were piled bows of every material, ash, and horn, and tougher fibres, with slackened strings, and among them peered a rusty clarion and battle-axe, while the quivers that should have accompanied lay in a distant corner, their arrows serving to pin long, dusty, torn banners to the wall. Opposite the entrance, an archer in bronze hung on tiptoe, and levelled a steel bow, whose piercing fleche seemed sparkling with impatience to spring from his finger and flesh itself in the heart of the intruder. The hauberk and halberd, lance and casque, arquebuse and sword, were suspended in friendly congeries; and fragments of costly stuff swept from ceiling to floor, crushed and soiled by the heaps of rusty firelocks, cutlasses, and gauntlets thrown upon them. In one place, a little antique bust was half hid in the folds of some pennon, still dyed with battle-stains; in another, scattered treasures of Dresden and Sevres brought the drawing-room into the campaign; and all around bivouacked rifles, whose polished barrels glittered full of death, — pistols, variously mounted, for an insurgent at the barricades, or for a lost millionnaire at the gaming-table, — foils, with buttoned bluntness, — and rapiers whose even edges were viewless as if filed into air. Destruction lay everywhere, at the command of the owner of this place, and, had he possessed a particle of vivacity, it would have been hazardous to bow beneath his doorway. It did not, I must say, look like a place where I should find a diamond. As the owner came forward, I determined on my plan of action.

"You have, sir," I said, handing him a bit of paper, on which were scrawled some numbers, "a diamond in your possession, of such and so many carats, size, and value, belonging to the Duke of X., and left with you by an Englishman, Mr. Arthur Ulster. You will deliver it to me, if you please."

"Monsieur!" exclaimed the man, lifting his hands, and surveying me with the widest eyes I ever saw. "A diamond! In my possession! So immense a thing! It is impossible. I have not even seen one of the kind. It is a mistake. Jacques Noailles, the vender of jewels en gros, second door below, must be the man. One should perceive that my business is with arms, not diamonds. I have it not; it would ruin me."

Here he paused for a reply, but, meeting none, resumed. "M. Arthur Ulster! — I have heard of no such person. I never spoke with an Englishman. Bah! I detest them! I have no dealings with them. I repeat, I have not your jewel. Do you wish anything more of me?"

His vehemence only convinced me of the truth of my suspicions.

"These heroics are out of place," I answered. "I demand the article in question."

"Monsieur doubts me?" he asked, with a rueful face, — "questions my word, which is incontrovertible?" Here he clapped his hand upon a couteau-de-chasse lying near, but, appearing to think better of it, drew himself up, and, with a shower of nods flung at me, added, "I deny your accusation!" I had not accused him.

"You are at too much pains to convict yourself. I charge you with nothing," I said. "But this diamond must be surrendered."

"Monsieur is mad!" he exclaimed, "mad! he dreams! Do I look like one who possesses such a trophy? Does my shop resemble a mine? Look about! See! All that is here would not bring a hundredth part of its price. I beseech Monsieur to believe me; he has mistaken the number, or has been misinformed."

"We waste words. I know this diamond is here, as well as a costly chain — "

"On my soul, on my life, on my honor," he cried clasping his hands and turning up his eyes, "there is here nothing of the kind. I do not deal in gems. A little silk, a few weapons, a curiosity, a nicknack, comprise my stock. I have not the diamond. I do not know the thing. I am poor. I am honest. Suspicion destroys me!"

"As you will find, should I be longer troubled by your denials."

He was inflexible, and, having exhausted every artifice of innocence, wiped the tears from his eyes, — oh, these French! life is their theatre, — and remained quiet. It was getting dark. There was no gas in the place; but in the pause a distant street-lamp swung its light dimly round.

"Unless one desires to purchase, allow me to say that it is my hour for closing," he remarked, blandly, rubbing his black-bearded chin.

"My time is valuable," I returned. "It is late and dark. When your shop-boy lights up — "

"Pardon, — we do not light."

"Permit me, then, to perform that office for you. In this blaze you may perceive my companions, whom you have not appeared to recognize."

So saying, I scratched a match upon the floor, and, as the sergent-de-ville and the gendarme advanced, threw the light of the blue spirit of sulphurous flame upon them. In a moment more the match went out, and we remained in the demi-twilight of the distant lantern. The marchand des armures stood petrified and aghast. Had he seen the imps of Satan in that instant, it could have had no greater effect.

"You have seen them?" I asked. "I regret to inconvenience you; but unless this diamond is produced at once, my friends will put their seal on your goods, your property will be confiscated, yourself in a dungeon. In other words, I allow you five minutes; at the close of that time you will have chosen between restitution and ruin."

He remained apparently lost in thought. He was a big, stout man, and with one blow his powerful fist could easily have settled me. It was the last thing in his mind. At length he lifted his head, — "Rosalie!" he called.

At the word, a light foot pattered along a stone floor within, and in a moment a little woman stood in an arch raised by two steps from our own level. Carrying a

candle, she descended and tripped toward him. She was
not pretty, but sprightly and keen, as the perpetual
attrition of life must needs make her, and wore the
everlasting grisette costume, which displays the neatest of
ankles, and whose cap is more becoming than wreaths of
garden millinery. I am too minute, I see, but it is second
nature. The two commenced a vigorous whispering amid
sundry gestures and glances. Suddenly the woman
turned, and, laying the prettiest of little hands on my
sleeve, said, with a winning smile, —

"Is it a crime of lèse-majesté?"

This was a new idea, but might be useful.

"Not yet," I said; "two minutes more, and I will not
answer for the consequence.'

Other whispers ensued.

"Monsieur," said the man, leaning on one arm over
the counter, and looking up in my face, with the most
engaging frankness, — "it is true that I have such a
diamond; but it is not mine. It is left with me to be
delivered to the Baron Stahl, who comes as an agent
from his court for its purchase."

"Yes, — I know."

"He was to have paid me half a million francs, — not half its worth, — in trust for the person who left it, who is not M. Arthur Ulster, but Mme. de St. Cyr."

Madame de St. Cyr! How under the sun — No, — it could not be possible. The case stood as it stood before. The rogue was in deeper water than I had thought; he had merely employed Mme. de St. Cyr. I ran this over in my mind, while I said, "Yes."

"Now, sir," I continued, "you will state the terms of this transaction."

"With pleasure. For my trouble I was myself to receive patronage and five thousand francs. The Baron is to be here directly, on other and public business. Reine du ciel, Monsieur! how shall I meet him?"

"He is powerless in Paris; your fear is idle."

"True. There were no other terms."

"Nor papers?"

"The lady thought it safest to be without them. She took merely my receipt, which the Baron Stahl will bring to me from her before receiving this."

"I will trouble you for it now."

He bowed and shuffled away. At a glance from me, the gendarme slipped to the rear of the building, where three others were stationed at the two exits in that direction, to caution them of the critical moment, and returned. Ten minutes passed, — the merchant did not appear. If, after all, he had made off with it! There had been the click of a bolt, the half-stifled rattle of arms, as if a door had been opened and rapidly closed again, but nothing more.

"I will see what detains my friend," said Mademoiselle, the little woman.

We suffered her to withdraw. In a moment more a quick expostulation was to be heard.

"They are there, the gendarmes, my little one! I should have run, but they caught me, the villains! and replaced me in the house. Oh, sacre!" — and rolling this word between his teeth, he came down and laid a little box on the counter. I opened it. There was within a large, glittering, curiously cut piece of glass. I threw it aside.

"The diamond!" I exclaimed.

"Monsieur had it," he replied, stooping to pick up the glass with every appearance of surprise and care.

"Do you mean to say you endeavored to escape with that bawble? Produce the diamond instantly, or you shall hang as high as Haman!" I roared.

Whether he knew the individual in question or not, the threat was efficient; he trembled and hesitated, and finally drew the identical shagreen case from his bosom.

"I but jested," he said. "Monsieur will witness that I relinquish it with reluctance."

"I will witness that you receive stolen goods!" I cried, in wrath.

He placed it in my hands.

"Oh!" he groaned, from the bottom of his heart, hanging his head, and laying both hands on the counter before him, — "it pains, it grieves me to part with it!"

"And the chain," I said.

"Monsieur did not demand that!"

"I demand it now."

In a moment, the chain also was given me.

"And now will Monsieur do me a favor? Will he inform me by what means he ascertained these facts?"

I glanced at the garcon, who had probably supplied himself with his masters finery illicitly; — he was the means; — we have some generosity; — I thought I should prefer doing him the favor, and declined.

I unclasped the shagreen case; the sergent-de-ville and the gendarme stole up and looked over my shoulder; the garcon drew near with round eyes; the little woman peeped across; the merchant, with tears streaming over his face, gazed as if it had been a loadstone; finally, I looked myself. There it lay, the glowing, resplendent thing! flashing in affluence of splendor, throbbing and palpitant with life, drawing all the light from the little woman's candle, from the sparkling armor around, from the steel barbs, and the distant lantern, into its bosom. It was scarcely so large as I had expected to see it, but more brilliant than anything I could conceive of. I do not believe there is another such in the world. One saw clearly that the Oriental superstition of the sex of stones was no fable; this was essentially the female of diamonds, the queen herself, the principle of life, the rejoicing receptive force. It was not radiant, as the term literally taken implies; it seemed rather to retain its wealth, — instead of emitting its glorious rays, to curl them back like the fringe of a madrepore, and lie there with redoubled quivering scintillations, a mass of white magnificence, not prismatic, but a vast milky lustre. I closed the case; on reopening it, I could scarcely believe that the beautiful sleepless eye would again flash upon me. I did not comprehend how it could afford such perpetual richness, such sheets of lustre.

At last we compelled ourselves to be satisfied. I left the shop, dismissed my attendants, and, fresh from the contemplation of this miracle, again trod the dirty, reeking streets, crossed the bridge, with its lights, its warehouses midway, its living torrents who poured on unconscious of the beauty within their reach. The thought of their ignorance of the treasure, not a dozen yards distant, has often made me question if we all are not equally unaware of other and greater processes of life, of more perfect, sublimed and, as it were, spiritual crystallizations going on invisibly about us. But had these been told of the thing clutched in the hand of a passer, how many of them would have know where to turn? and we, — are we any better?

II

FOR a few days I carried the diamond about my person, and did not mention its recovery even to my valet, who knew that I sought it, but communicated only with the Marquis of G., who replied, that he would be in Paris on a certain day, when I could safely deliver it to him.

It was now generally rumored that the neighboring government was about to send us the Baron Stahl, ambassador concerning arrangements for a loan to maintain the sinking monarchy in supremacy at Paris, the usual synecdoche for France.

The weather being fine, I proceeded to call on Mme. de St. Cyr. She received me in her boudoir, and on my way thither I could not but observe the perfect quiet and cloistered seclusion that prevaded the whole house, — the house itself seeming only an adjunct of the still and sunny garden, of which one caught a glimpse through the long open hall- windows beyond. This boudoir did not differ from others to which I have been admitted: the same delicate shades; all the dainty appliances of Art for beauty; the lavish profusion of bijouterie; and the usual statuettes of innocence, to indicate, perhaps, the presence of that commodity which might not be guessed at otherwise; and burning in a silver cup, a rich perfume loaded the air with voluptuous sweetness. Through a half-open door an inner boudoir was to be seen, which must have been Delphine's; it looked like her; the prevailing hue was a soft purple, or gray; a prie-dieu, a bookshelf, and desk, of a dark West Indian wood, were just visible. There was but one picture, — a sad-eyed, beautiful Fate. It was the type of her nation. I think she worshipped it. And how apt is misfortune to degenerate into Fate! — not that the girl had ever experienced the former, but, dissatisfied with life, and seeing no outlet, she accepted it stoically and waited till it should be over. She needed to be aroused; — the station of an ambassadrice, which I desired for her, might kindle the spark. There were no flowers, no perfumes, no busts, in this ascetic place. Delphine herself, in some faint rosy gauze, her fair hair streaming round her, as she lay on a white-draped couch, half-risen on one arm, while she read the morning's feuilleton, was the most perfect statuary of which a room could boast, — illumined, as I saw her, by the gay beams that entered at the loftily-arched window, broken only by the flickering of the vine-leaves that clustered the curiously-latticed panes without. She resembled in kind a Nymph, just bursting from the sea; so Pallas might have posed for Aphrodite. Madame de St. Cyr received me with empressement, and, so doing, closed the door of this shrine. We spoke of various things, — of the court, the theatre, the weather, the world, — skating lightly round the slender edges of her secret, till finally she invited me to lunch with her in the garden. Here, on a rustic table, stood wine and a few delicacies, — while, by extending a hand, we could grasp the hanging pears and nectarines, still warm to the lip and luscious with sunshine, as we disputed possession with the envious wasp who had established a priority of claim.

"It is to be hoped," I said, sipping the Haut-Brion, whose fine and brittle smack contrasted rarely with the delicious juiciness of the fruit, "that you have laid in a supply of this treasure that neither moth nor rust doth corrupt, before parting with that little gem in the Gironde."

"Ah? You know, then, that I have sold it?"

"Yes," I replied. "I have the pleasure of Mr. Ulster's acquaintance."

"He arranged the terms for me," she said, with restraint, — adding, "I could almost wish now that it had not been."

This was probably true; for the sum which she hoped to receive from Ulster for standing sponsor to his jewel was possibly equal to the price of her vineyard.

"It was indispensable at the time, this sale; I thought best to hazard it on one more season. — If, after such advantages, Delphine will not marry, why — it remains to retire into the country and end our days with the barbarians!" she continued, shrugging her shoulders; "I have a house there."

"But you will not be obliged to throw us all into despair by such a step now," I replied.

She looked quickly, as if to see how nearly I had approached her citadel, — then, finding in my face no expression but a complimentary one, "No," she said, "I hope that my affairs have brightened a little. One never knows what is in store."

Before long I had assured myself that Mme. de St. Cyr was not a party to the theft, but had merely been hired by Ulster, who, discovering the state of her affairs, had not, therefore, revealed his own, — and this without in the least implying any knowledge on my part of the transaction. Ulster must have seen the necessity of leaving the business in the hands of a competent person, and Mme. de St. Cyr's financial talent was patent. There were few ladies in Paris who would have rejected the opportunity. Of these things I felt a tolerable certainty.

"We throng with foreigners," said Madame, archly, as I reached this point. "Diplomates, too. The Baron Stahl arrives in a day."

"I have heard," I responded. "You are acquainted?"

"Alas! no," she said. "I knew his father well, though he himself is not young. Indeed, the families thought once of intermarriage. But nothing has been said on the subject for many years. His Excellency, I hear, will strengthen himself at home by an alliance with the young Countess, the natural daughter of the Emperor."

"He surely will never be so imprudent as to rivet his chain by such a link!"

"It is impossible to compute the dice in those despotic countries," she rejoined, — which was pretty well, considering the freedom enjoyed by France at that period.

"It may be," I suggested, "that the Baron hopes to open this delicate subject with you yourself, Madame."

"It is unlikely," she said, sighing. "And for Delphine, should I tell her his excellency preferred scarlet, she would infallibly wear blue. Imagine her, Monsieur, in fine scarlet, with a scarf of gold gauze, and rustling grasses in that unruly gold hair of hers! She would be divine!"

The maternal instinct as we have it here at Paris confounds me. I do not comprehend it. Here was a mother who did not particularly love her child, who would not be inconsolable at her loss, would not ruin her own complexion by care of her during illness, would send her through fire and water and every torture to secure or maintain a desirable rank, who yet would entangle herself deeply in intrigue, would not hesitate to tarnish her own reputation, and would, in fact, raise heaven and earth to — endow this child with a brilliant match. And Mme. de St. Cyr seemed to regard Delphine, still further, as a cool matter of Art.

These little confidences, moreover, are provoking. They put you yourself so entirely out of the question.

"Mlle. de St. Cyr's beauty is peerless," I said, slightly chagrined, and at a loss. "If hearts were trumps, instead of diamonds!"

"We are poor," resumed Madame, pathetically. "Delphine is not an heiress. Delphine is proud. She will not stoop to charm. Her coquetry is that of an Amazon. Her kisses are arrows. She is Medusa!" And Madame, her mother, shivered.

Here, with her hair knotted up and secured by a tiny dagger, her gauzy drapery gathered in her arm, Delphine floated down the green alley toward us, as if in a rosy cloud. But this soft aspect never could have been more widely contradicted than by the stony repose and cutting calm of her beautiful face.

"The Marquis of G.," said her mother, "he also arrives ambassador. Has he talent? Is he brilliant? Wealthy, of course, — but gauche?"

Therewith I sketched for them the Marquis and his surroundings.

"It is charming," said Madame. "Delphine, do you attend?"

"And why?" asked Delphine, half concealing a yawn with her dazzling hand. "It is wearisome; it matters not to me."

"But he will not go to marry himself in France," said her mother. "Oh, these English," she added, with a laugh, "yourself, Monsieur, being proof of it, will not mingle blood, lest the Channel should still flow between the little red globules! You will go? but to return shortly? You will dine with me soon? Au revoir!" and she gave me her hand graciously, while Delphine bowed as if I were already gone, threw herself into a garden-chair, and commenced pouring the wine on a stone for a little tame snake which came out and lapped it.

Such women as Mme. de St. Cyr have a species of magnetism about them. It is difficult to retain one's self-respect before them, — for no other reason than that one is, at the moment, absorbed into their individuality, and thinks and acts with them. Delphine must have had a strong will, and perpetual antagonism did not weaken it. As for me, Madame had, doubtless, reasons of her own for tearing aside these customary bands of reserve — reasons which, if you do not perceive, I shall not enumerate.

III

"HAVE YOU MET WITH anything further in your search, sir?" asked my valet next morning.

"Oh, yes, Hay," I returned, in a very good humor, — "with great success. You have assisted me so much, that I am sure I owe it to you to say that I have found the diamond."

"Indeed, sir, you are very kind. I have been interested, but my assistance is not worth mentioning. I thought likely it might be, you appeared so quiet." — The cunning dog! — "How did you find it, sir, may I ask?"

I briefly related the leading facts, since he had been aware of the progress of the case to that point, — without, however, mentioning Mme. de St. Cyr's name.

"And Monsieur did not inform us!" a French valet would have cried.

"You were prudent not to mention it, sir," said Hay. "These walls must have better ears than ordinary; for a family has moved in on the first floor recently, whose actions are extremely suspicious. But is this precious affair to be seen?"

I took it from an inner pocket and displayed it, having discarded the shagreen case as inconvenient.

"His Excellency must return as he came," said I.

Hay's eyes sparkled.

"And do you carry it there, sir?" he asked, with surprise, as I restored it to my waistcoat-pocket.

"I shall take it to the bank," I said. "I do not like the responsibility."

"It is very unsafe," was the warning of this cautious fellow. "Why, sir! any of these swells, these pickpockets, might meet you, run against you, — so!" said Hay, suiting the action to the word," and, with the little sharp knife concealed in just such a ring as this I wear, give a light tap, and there's a slit in your vest sir, but no diamond!" — and instantly resuming his former respectful deportment, Hay handed me my gloves and stick, and smoothed my hat.

"Nonsense!" I replied, drawing on the gloves, "I should like to see the man who could be too quick for me. Any news from India, Hay?"

"None of consequence, sir. The indigo crop is said to have failed which advances the figure of that on hand, so that one or two fortunes will be made to-day. Your hat, sir? — your lunettes? Here they are, sir."

"Good morning, Hay."

"Good morning, sir."

I descended the stairs, buttoning my gloves, paused a moment at the door to look about, and proceeded down the street, which was not more than usually thronged. At the bank I paused to assure myself that the diamond was safe. My fingers caught in a singular slit. I started. As Hay had prophesied there was a fine longitudinal cut in my waistcoat, but the pocket was empty. My God! the thing was gone. I never can forget the blank nihility of all existence that dreadful moment when I stood fumbling for what was not. Calm as I sit here and tell of it, I vow to you a shiver courses through me at the very thought. I had circumvented Stahl only to destroy myself. The diamond was lost again. My mind flew like lightning over every chance, and a thousand started up like steel spikes to snatch the bolt. For a moment I was stunned, but, never being very subject to despair, on my recovery, which was almost at once, took every measure that could be devised. Who had touched me? Whom had I met? Through what streets had I come? In ten minutes the Prefect had the matter in hand. My injunctions were strict privacy. I sincerely hoped the mishap would not reach England; and if the diamond were not recovered before the Marquis of G. arrived, — why, there was the Seine. It is all very well to talk, — yet suicide is so French an affair, that an Englishman does not take to it naturally, and, except in November, the Seine is too cold and damp for comfort, but during that month I suppose it does not greatly differ in these respects from our own atmosphere.

A preternatural activity now possessed me. I slept none, ate little, worked immoderately. I spared no efforts, for everything was at stake. In the midst of all, G. arrived. Hay also exerted himself to the utmost; I promised him a hundred pounds, if I found it. He never told me that he said how it would be, never intruded the state of the market, never resented my irritating conduct, but watched me with narrow yet kind solicitude, and frequently offered valuable suggestions, which, however, as everything else did, led to nothing. I did not call on G., but in a week or so his card was brought up one morning to me. "Deny me," I groaned. It yet wanted a week of the day on which I had promised to deliver him the diamond Meanwhile the Baron Stahl had reached Paris, but he still remained in private, — few had seen him.

The police were forever on the wrong track. Today they stopped the old Comptesse du Quesne and her jewels, at the Barriere; to-morrow, with their long needles, they riddled a package of lace destined for the Duchess of X. herself; the Secret Service was doubled; and to crown all, a splendid new star of the testy Prince de Ligne was examined and proclaimed to be paste, — the Prince swearing vengeance, if he could discover the cause, — while half Paris must have been under arrest. My own hotel was ransacked thoroughly, — Hay begging that his traps might be included, — but nothing resulted, and I expected nothing, for, of course, I could swear that the stone was in my pocket when I stepped into the street. I confess I never was nearer madness, — every word and gesture stung me like asps, — I walked on burning coals. Enduring all this torment, I must yet meet my daily comrades, eat ices at Tortoni's, stroll on the Boulevards, call on my acquaintance, with the same equanimity as before. I believe I was equal to it. Only by contrast with that blessed time when Ulster and diamonds were unknown, could I imagine my past happiness, my present wretchedness. Rather than suffer it again, I would be stretched on the rack till ever! bone in my skin were broken. I cursed Mr. Arthur Ulster every hour in the day; myself, as well; and even now the word diamond sends a cold blast to my heart. I often met my friend the marchand des armures. It was his turn to triumph; I fancied there must be a hang-dog kind of air about me, as about every sharp man who has been outwitted. It wanted finally but two days of that on which I was to deliver the diamond.

One midnight, armed with a dark lantern and a cloak, I was traversing the streets alone, — unsuccessful, as usual, just now solitary, and almost in despair. As I turned a corner, two men were but scarcely visible a step before me. It was a badly-lighted part of the town. Unseen and noiseless I followed. They spoke in low tones, — almost whispers; or rather, one spoke, — the other seemed to nod assent.

"On the day but one after to-morrow," I heard spoken in English. Great Heavens! was it possible? had I arrived at a clew? That was the day of days for me. "You have given it, you say, in this billet, — I wish to be exact, you see," continued the voice, — "to prevent detection, you gave it, ten minutes after it came into your hands, to the butler of Madame ," (here the speaker stumbled on the rough pavement, and I lost the name,) "who," he continued, "will put it in the —" (a second stumble acted like a hiccough) "cellar."

"Wine-cellar," I thought; "and what then?"

"In the ——." A third stumble was followed by a round German oath. How easy it is for me now to fill up the little blanks which that unhappy pavement caused!

"You share your receipts with this butler. On the day I obtain it," he added, and I now perceived his foreign accent, "I hand you one hundred thousand francs; afterward, monthly payments till you have received the stipulated sum. But how will this butler know me, in season to prevent a mistake? Hem! — he might give it to the other!"

My hearing had been trained to such a degree that I would have promised to catch any given dialogue of the spirits themselves, but the whisper that answered him eluded me. I caught nothing but a faint sibillation. "Your ring?" was the rejoinder. "He shall be instructed to recognize it? Very well. It is too large, — no, that will do, it fits the first finger. There is nothing more. I am under infinite obligations, sir; they shall be remembered. Adieu!"

The two parted; which should I pursue? In desperation I turned my lantern upon one, and illumined a face fresh with color, whose black eyes sparkled askance after the retreating figure, under straight black brows. In a moment more he was lost in a false cul-de-sac, and I found it impossible to trace the other.

I was scarcely better off than before; but it seemed to me that I had obtained something, and that now it was wisest to work this vein. "The butler of Madame — —." There were hundreds of thousands of Madames in town. I might call on all, and he as old as the Wandering Jew at the last call. The cellar. Wine-cellar, of course, — that came by a natural connection with butler, — but whose? There was one under my own abode; certainly I would explore it. Meanwhile, let us see the entertainments for Wednesday. The Prefect had a list of these. For some I found I had cards; I determined to allot a fraction of time to as many as possible; my friends in the Secret Service would divide the labor. Among others, Madame de St. Cyr gave a dinner, and, as she had been in the affair, I determined not to neglect her on this occasion, although having no definite idea of what had been, or plan of what should be done. I decided not to speak of this occurrence to Hay, since it might only bring him off some trail that he had struck.

Having been provided with keys, early on the following evening I entered the wine-cellar, and, concealed in an empty cask that would have held a dozen of me, waited for something to turn up. Really, when I think of myself, a diplomate, a courtier, a man-about-town, curled in a dusty, musty wine-barrel, I am moved with vexation and laughter. Nothing, however, turned up, — and at length I retired baffled. The next night came, — no news, no identification of my black-browed man, no success; but I felt certain that something must transpire in that cellar. I don't know why I had pitched upon that one in particular, but, at an earlier hour than on the previous night, I again donned the cask. A long time must have elapsed; dead silence filled the spacious vaults, except where now and then some Sillery cracked the air with a quick explosion, or some newer wine bubbled round the bung of its barrel with a faint effervescence. I had no intention of leaving this place till morning, but it suddenly appeared like the most woeful waste of time. The master of this tremendous affair should be abroad and active; who knew what his keen eyes might detect; what loss his absence might occasion in this nick of time? And here he was, shut up and locked in a wine-cellar! I began to be very nervous; I had already, with aid, searched every crevice of the cellar; and now I thought it would be some consolation to discover the thief, if I never regained the diamond. A distant clock tolled midnight. There was a faint noise, — a mouse? — no, it was too prolonged; — nor did it sound like the fiz of Champagne; — a great iron door was turning on its hinges; a man with a lantern was entering; another followed, and another. They seated themselves. In a few moments, appearing one by one and at intervals, some thirty people were in the cellar. Were they all to share in the proceeds of the diamond? With what jaundiced eye we behold things! I myself saw all that was only through the lens of this diamond, of which not one of these men had ever heard. As the lantern threw its feeble glimmer on this group, and I surveyed them through my loophole, I thought I had never seen so wild and savage a picture, such enormous shadows, such bold outline, such a startling flash on the face of their leader, such light retreating up the threatening arches. More resolute brows, more determined words, more unshrinking hearts, I had not met. In fact, I found myself in the centre of a conspiracy, a society as vindictive as the Jacobins, as unknown and terrible as the Marianne of to-day. I was thunderstruck, too, at the countenances on which the light fell, — men the loyalest in estimation, ministers and senators, millionnaires who had no reason for discontent, dandies whose reason was supposed to be devoted to their tailors, poets and artists of generous aspiration and suspected tendencies, and one woman, — Delphine de St. Cyr. Their plans were brave, their determination lofty, their conclave serious and fine; yet as slowly they shut up their hopes and fears in the black masks, one man bent toward the lantern to adjust his. When he lifted his face before concealing it, I recognized him also. I had met him frequently at the Bureau of Police; he was, I believe, Secretary of the Secret Service.

I had no sympathy with these people. I had sufficient liberty myself, I was well enough satisfied with the world, I did not care to revolutionize France; but my heart rebelled at the mockery, as this traitor and spy, this creature of a system by which I gained my fame, showed his revolting face and veiled it again. And Delphine, what had she to do with them? One by one, as they entered, they withdrew, and I was left alone again. But all this was not my diamond.

Another hour elapsed. Again the door opened, and remained ajar. Some one entered, whom I could not see. There was a pause, — then a rustle, — the door creaked ever so little. "Art thou there?" lisped a shrill whisper, — a woman, as I could guess.

"My angel, it is I," was returned, a semitone lower. She approached, he advanced, and the consequence was a salute resonant as the smack with which a Dutch burggomaster may be supposed to set down his mug. I was prepared for anything. Ye gods! if it should be Delphine! But the base suspicion was birth-strangled as they spoke again. The conversation which now ensued between these lovers under difficulties was tender and affecting beyond expression. I had felt guilty enough when an unwilling auditor of the conspirators, — since, though one employs spies, one does not therefore act that part one's self, but on emergencies, — an unwillingness which would not, however, prevent my turning to advantage the information gained; but here, to listen to this rehearsal of woes and blisses, this ah mon Fernand, this aria in an area, growing momently more fervent, was too much I overturned the cask, scrambled upon my feet, and fled from the cellar leaving the astounded lovers to follow, while, agreeably to my instincts and regardless of the diamond, I escaped the embarrassing predicament.

At length it grew to be noon of the appointed day. Nothing had transpired; all our labor was idle. I felt, nevertheless, more buoyant than usual, — whether because I was now to put my fate to the test, or that today was the one of which my black-browed man had spoken, and I therefore entertained a presentiment of good fortune, I cannot say. But when, in unexceptionable toilet, I stood on Mme. de St. Cyr's steps, my heart sunk. G. was doubtless already within, and I thought of the marchand des armures' exclamation, "Queen of Heaven, Monsieur! how shall I meet him!" I was plunged at once into the profoundest gloom. Why had I undertaken the business at all? This interference, this good-humor, this readiness to oblige, — it would ruin me yet! I forswore it, as Falstaff forswore honor. Why needed I to meddle in the melee? Why — But I was no catechumen. Questions were useless now. My emotions are not chronicled on my face, I flatter myself; and with my usual repose I saluted our hostess. Greeting G. without any allusion to the diamond, the absence of which allusion he received as a point of etiquette, I was conversing with Mrs. Leigh, when the Baron Stahl was announced. I turned to look at his Excellency. A glance electrified me. There was my dark-browed man of the midnight streets. It must, then, have been concerning the diamond that I had heard him speak. His countenance, his eager glittering eye, told that to-day was as eventful to him as to me. If he were here, I could well afford to be. As he addressed me in English, my certainty was confirmed; and the instant in which I observed the ring, gaudy and coarse, upon his finger, made confirmation doubly sure. I own I was surprised that anything could induce the Baron to wear such an ornament. Here he was actually risking his reputation as a man of taste, as an exquisite, a leader of haut ton, a gentleman, by the detestable vulgarity of this ring. But why do I speak so of the trinket? Do I not owe it a thrill of as fine joy as I ever knew? Faith! it was not unfamiliar to me. It had been a daily sight for years. In meeting the Baron Stahl I had found the diamond.

The Baron Stahl was then, the thief? Not at all. My valet, as of course you have been all along aware, was the thief.

My valet, moreover, was my instructor; he taught me not again to scour Cathay for what might be lying under my hand at home. Nor have I since been so acute as to overreach myself. Yet I can explain such intolerable stupidity only by remembering that when one has been in the habit of pointing his telescope at the stars, he is not apt to turn it upon pebbles at his feet.

The Marquis of G. took down Mme. de St. Cyr; Stahl preceded me, with Delphine. As we sat at table, G. was at the right, I at the left of our hostess Next G. sat Delphine; below her, the Baron; so that we were nearly vis-à-vis. I was now as fully convinced that Mme. de St. Cyr's cellar was the one, as the day before I had been that the other was; I longed to reach it. Hay had given the stone to a butler — doubtless this — the moment of its theft; but, not being aware of Mme. de St. Cyr's previous share in the adventure, had probably not afforded her another. And thus I concluded her to be ignorant of the game we were about to play; and I imagined, with the interest that one carries into a romance, the little preliminary scene between the Baron and Madame that must have already taken place, being charmed by the cheerfulness with which she endured the loss of the promised reward.

As the Baron entered the dining-room, I saw him withdraw his glove, and move the jewelled hand across his hair while passing the solemn butler, who gave it a quick recognition; — the next moment we were seated. There were only wines on the table, clustered around a central ornament, — a bunch of tall silver rushes and flagleaves, on whose airy tip danced fleurs-de-lis of frosted silver, a design of Delphine's, — the dishes being on sidetables, from which the guests were served as they signified their choice of the variety on their cards. Our number not being large, and the custom so informal, rendered it pleasant.

I had just finished my oysters and was pouring out a glass of Chablis, when another plate was set before the Baron.

"His Excellency has no salt," murmured the butler, — at the same time placing one beside him. A glance, at entrance, had taught me that most of the service was uniform; this dainty little saliere I had noticed on the buffet, solitary, and unlike the others. What a fool had I been! Those gaps in the Baron's remarks caused by the pavingstones, how easily were they to be supplied!

"Madame?"

Madame de St. Cyr.

"The cellar?"

A salt-cellar.

How quick the flash that enlightened me while I surveyed the saliere!

"It is exquisite! Am I never to sit at your table but some new device charms me?" I exclaimed. "Is it your design, Mademoiselle?" I said, turning to Delphine.

Delphine, who had been ice to all the Baron's advances, only curled her lip. "Des babioles!" she said.

"Yes, indeed!" cried Mme. de St. Cyr, extending her hand for it. "But none the less her taste. Is it not a fairy thing? À Cellini! Observe this curve, these lines! but one man could have drawn them!" — and she held it for our scrutiny. It was a tiny hand and arm of ivory, parting the foam of a wave and holding a golden shell, in which the salt seemed to have crusted itself as if in some secretest ocean-hollow. I looked at the Baron a moment; his eyes were fastened upon the saliere, and all the color had forsaken his cheeks, — his face counted his years. The diamond was in that little shell. But how to obtain it? I had no novice to deal with; nothing but finesse would answer.

"Permit me to examine it?" I said. She passed it to her left hand for me to take. The butler made a step forward.

"Meanwhile, Madame," said the Baron, smiling, "I have no salt."

The instinct of hospitality prevailed; — she was about to return it. Might I do an awkward thing? Unhesitatingly. Reversing my glass, I gave my arm a wider sweep than necessary, and, as it met her hand with violence, the saliere fell. Before it touched the floor I caught it. There was still a pinch of salt left, — nothing more.

"A thousand pardons!" I said, and restored it to the Baron.

His Excellency beheld it with dismay; it was rare to see him bend over and scrutinize it with starting eyes.

"Do you find there what Count Arnaldos begs in the song," asked Delphine, — "the secret of the sea, Monsieur?"

He handed it to the butler, observing, "I find here no — "

"Salt, Monsieur?" replied the man, who did not doubt but all had gone right, and replenished it.

Had one told me in the morning, that no intricate manœuvres, but a simple blunder, would effect this, I might have met him in the Bois de Boulogne.

"We will not quarrel," said my neighbor, lightly, with reference to the popular superstition

"Rather propitiate the offended deities by a crumb tossed over the shoulder," added I.

"Over the left?" asked the Baron, to intimate his knowledge of another idiom, together with a reproof for my gauchene.

"A gauche, — quelquefois c'est justement a droit, " I replied.

"Salt in any pottage," said Madame, a little uneasily, "is like surprise in an individual; it brings out the flavor of every ingredient, so my cook tells me."

"It is a preventive of palsy," I remarked, as the slight trembling of my adversary's finger caught my eye.

"And I have noticed that a taste for it is peculiar to those who trace their blood," continued Madame.

"Let us, therefore, elect a deputation to those mines near Cracow," said Delphine.

"To our cousins, the slaves there?" laughed her mother.

"I must vote to lay your bill on the table, Mademoiselle," I rejoined.

"But with a boule blanche, Monsieur?"

"As the salt has been laid on the floor," said the Baron.

Meanwhile, as this light skirmishing proceeded, my sleeve and Mme. de St. Cyr's dress were slightly powdered, but I had not seen the diamond. The Baron, bolder than I, looked under the table, but made no discovery. I was on the point of dropping my napkin to accomplish a similar movement when my accommodating neighbor dropped hers. To restore it, I stooped. There it lay, large and glowing, the Sea of Splendor, the Moon of Milk, the Torment of my Life, on the carpet, within half an inch of a lady's slipper Mademoiselle de St. Cyr's foot had prevented the Baron from seeing it; now it moved and unconsciously covered it. All was as I wished. I hastily restored the napkin, and looked steadily at Delphine, — so steadily, that she perceived some meaning, as she had already suspected a game. By my sign she understood me, pressed her foot upon the stone and drew it nearer. In France we do not remain at table until unfit for a lady's society, — we rise with them. Delphine needed to drop neither napkin nor handkerchief; she composedly stooped and picked up the stone, so quickly at no one saw what it was.

"And the diamond?" said the Baron to the butler, rapidly, as he passed.

"It was in the saliere," whispered the astonished creature.

IV

IN THE DRAWING-ROOM I sought the Marquis.

"To-day I was to surrender you your property," I said; "it is here."

"Do you know," he replied, "I thought I must have been mistaken?"

"Any of our volatile friends here might have been," I resumed; "for us it is impossible. Concerning this, when you return to France, I will relate the incidents; at present, there are those who will not hesitate to take life to obtain its possession. A conveyance leaves in twenty minutes; and if I owned the diamond, it should not leave me behind. Moreover, who knows what a day may bring forth? To-morrow there may be an émeute. Let me restore the thing as you withdraw."

The Marquis, who is not, after all, the Lion of England, pausing a moment to transmit my words from his ear to his brain, did not afterward delay to make inquiries or adieux, but went to seek Mme. de St. Cyr and wish her good-night, on his departure from Paris. As I awaited his return, which I knew would not be immediate, Delphine left the Baron and joined me.

"You beckoned me?" she asked.

"No, I did not."

"Nevertheless, I come by your desire, I am sure."

"Mademoiselle," I said, "I am not in the custom of doing favors; I have forsworn them. But before you return me my jewel, I risk my head and render one last one, and to you."

"Do not, Monsieur, at such price," she responded, with a slight mocking motion of her hand.

"Delphine! those resolves, last night, in the cellar, were daring, the were noble, yet they were useless."

She had not started, but a slight tremor ran over her person and vanished while I spoke.

"They will be allowed to proceed no farther, — the axe is sharpened; for the last man who adjusted his mask was a spy, — was the Secretary of the Secret Service

Delphine could not have grown paler than was usual with her of late. She flashed her eye upon me.

"He was, it may be, Monsieur himself," she said.

"I do not claim the honor of that post."

"But you were there, nevertheless, — a spy!"

"Hush, Delphine! It would be absurd to quarrel. I was there for the recovery of this stone, having heard that it was in a cellar, — when, stupidly enough, I had insisted should be a wine-cellar."

"It was, then — "

"In a salt-cellar, — a blunder which, as you do not speak English, you cannot comprehend. I never mix with treason, and did not wish to assist at your pastimes. I speak now, that you may escape."

"If Monsieur betrays his friends, the police, why should I expect a kinder fate?"

"When I use the police, they are my servants, not my friends. I simply warn you, that, before sunrise, you will be safer travelling than sleeping, — safer next week in Vienna than in Paris."

"Thank you! And the intelligence is the price of the diamond? If I had not chanced to pick it up, my throat," and she clasped it with her fingers, "had been no slenderer than the others?"

"Delphine, will you remember, should you have occasion to do so in Vienna, that it is just possible for an Englishman to have affections, and sentiments, and, in fact, sensations? that, with him, friendship can be inviolate, and to betray it an impossibility? And even were it not, I, Mademoiselle have not the pleasure to be classed by you as a friend."

"You err. I esteem Monsieur highly."

I was impressed by her coolness.

"Let me see if you comprehend the matter," I demanded.

"Perfectly. The arrest will be used to-night, the guillotine tomorrow."

"You will take immediate measures for flight?"

"No, — I do not see that life has value. I shall be the debtor of him who takes it."

"A large debt. Delphine, I exact a promise of you. I do not care to have endangered myself for nothing. It is not ù worth while to make your mother unhappy. Life is not yours to throw away. I appeal to your magnanimity."

"'Affections, sentiments, sensations!'" she quoted. "Your own danger for the affection, — it is an affair of the heart! Mme. de St. Cyr's unhappiness, — there is the sentiment. You are angry, Monsieur, — that must be the sensation."

"Delphine, I am waiting."

"Ah, well. You have mentioned Vienna, — and why? Liberals are countenanced there?"

"Not in the least. But Madame l'Ambassadrice will be countenanced.'

"I do not know her."

"We are not apt to know ourselves."

"Monsieur, how idle are these cross-purposes!" she said, folding her fan.

"Delphine," I continued, taking the fan, "tell me frankly which of these two men you prefer, — the Marquis or his Excellency."

"The Marquis? He is antiphlogistic, — he is ice. Why should I freeze myself? I am frozen now, — I need fire!"

Her eyes burned as she spoke, and a faint red flushed her cheek.

"Mademoiselle, you demonstrate to me that life has yet a value to you."

"I find no fire," she said, as the flush fell away.

"The Baron?"

"I do not affect him."

"You will conquer your prejudice in Vienna."

"I do not comprehend you, Monsieur; — you speak in riddles, which I do not like."

"I will speak plainer. But first let me ask you for the diamond."

"The diamond? It is yours? How am I certified of it? I find it on the floor; you say it was in my mother's salière; it is her affair, not mine. No, Monsieur, I do not see that the thing is yours."

Certainly there was nothing to be done but to relate the story, which I did, carefully omitting the Baron's name. At its conclusion, she placed the prize in my hand.

"Pardon, Monsieur." she said; "without doubt you should receive it. And this agent of the government, — one could turn him like hot iron in this vice, — who was he?"

"The Baron Stahl."

All this time G. had been waiting on thorns, and, leaving her now, I approached him, displayed for an instant the treasure on my palm, and slipped it into his. It was done. I bade farewell to this Eye of Morning and Heart of Day, this thing that had caused me such pain and perplexity and pleasure, with less envy and more joy than I thought myself capable of. The relief and buoyancy that seized me, as his hand closed upon it, I shall not attempt to portray. An abdicated king was not freer.

The Marquis departed, and I, wandering round the salon, was next stranded upon the Baron. He was yet hardly sure of himself. We talked indifferently for a few moments, and then I ventured on the great loan. He was, as became him, not communicative, but scarcely thought it would be arranged. I then spoke of Delphine.

"She is superb!" said the Baron, staring at her boldly.

She stood opposite, and, in her white attire on the background of the blue curtain, appeared like an impersonation of Greek genius relieved upon the blue of an Athenian heaven. Her severe and classic outline, her pallor, her downcast lids, her absorbed look, only heightened the resemblance. Her reverie seemed to end abruptly, the same red stained her cheek again, her lips curved in a proud smile, she raised her glowing eyes and observed us regarding her. At too great distance to hear our words, she quietly repaid our glances in the strength of her new decision, and then, turning, began to entertain those next her with an unwonted spirit.

"She has needed," I replied to the Baron, "but one thing, — to be aroused, to be kindled. See, it is done! I have thought that a life of cabinets and policy might achieve this, for her talent is second not even to her beauty."

"It is unhappy that both should be wasted," said the Baron. "She, of course, will never marry."

"Why not?"

"For various reasons."

"One?"

"She is poor."

"Which will not signify to your Excellency. Another?"

"She is too beautiful. One would fall in love with her. And to love one's own wife — it is ridiculous!"

"Who should know?" I asked.

"All the world would suspect and laugh."

"Let those laugh that win."

"No, — she would never do as a wife; but then as ____"

"But then in France we do not insult hospitality!"

The Baron transferred his gaze to me for a moment, then tapped his snuff-box, and approached the circle round Delphine.

It was odd that we, the arch enemies of the hour, could speak without the intervention of seconds; but I hoped that the Baron's conversation might be diverting, — the Baron hoped that mine might be didactic.

They were very gay with Delphine. He leaned on the back of a chair and listened. One spoke of the new gallery of the Tuileries, and the five pavilions, — a remark which led us to architecture.

"We all build our own houses," said Delphine, at last, "and then complain that they cramp us here, and the wind blows in there, while the fault is not in the order, but in us, who increase here and shrink there without reason."

"You speak in metaphors," said the Baron.

"Precisely. A truth is often more visible veiled than nude."

"We should soon exhaust the orders," I interposed; "for who builds like his neighbor?"

"Slight variations, Monsieur! Though we take such pains to conceal the style, it is not difficult to tell the order of architecture chosen by the builders in this room. My mother, for instance — you perceive that her pavilion would be the florid Gothic."

"Mademoiselle's is the Doric," I said.

"Has been," she murmured, with a quick glance.

"And mine, Mademoiselle?" asked the Baron, indifferently.

"Ah, Monsieur," she returned, looking serenely upon him, "when one has all the winning cards in hand and yet loses the stake, we allot him un pavillon chinois." — which was the polite way of dubbing him Court Fool.

The Baron's eyes fell. Vexation and alarm were visible on his contracted brow. He stood in meditation for some time. It must have been evident to him that Delphine knew of the recent occurrences, — that here in Paris she could denounce him as the agent of a felony, the participant of a theft. What might prevent it? Plainly but one thing: no woman would denounce her husband. He had scarcely contemplated this step on arrival.

The guests were again scattered in groups round the room. I examined an engraving on an adjacent table. Delphine reclined as lazily in a fauteuil as if her life did not hang in the balance. The Baron drew near.

"Mademoiselle," said he, "you allotted me just now a cap and bells. If two should wear it? — if I should invite another into my pavillon chinois? — if I should propose to complete an alliance, desired by my father, with the ancient family of St. Cyr? — if, in short, Mademoiselle, I should request you to become my wife?"

"Eh, bien, Monsieur, — and if you should?" I heard her coolly reply.

But it was no longer any business of mine. I rose and sought Mme. de St. Cyr, who, I thought, was slightly uneasy, perceiving some mystery to be afloat. After a few words, I retired.

Archimedes, as perhaps you have never heard, needed only a lever to move the world. Such a lever I had put into the hands of Delphine, with which she might move, not indeed the grand globe, with its multiplied attractions, relations, and affinities, but the lesser world of circumstances, of friends and enemies, the circle of hopes, fears, ambitions. There is no woman, as I believe, but could have used it.

V

THE NEXT DAY was scarcely so quiet in the city as usual. The great loan had not been negotiated. Both the Baron Stahl and the English minister had left Paris, — and there was a coup d'état.

But the Baron did not travel alone. There had been a ceremony at midnight in the Church of St. Sulpice, and her excellency the Baroness Stahl, nee de St. Cyr, accompanied him.

It is a good many years since. I have seen the diamond in the Duchess of X.'s coronet, once, when a young queen put on her royalty, — but I have never seen Delphine. The Marquis begged me to retain the chain, and I gave myself the pleasure of presenting it, through her mother, to the Baroness Stahl. I hear, that, whenever she desires to effect any cherished object which the Baron opposes, she has only to wear this chain, and effect it. It appears to possess a magical power, and its potent spell enslaves the Baron as the lamp and ring of Eastern tales enslaved the Afrites. The life she leads has aroused her. She is no longer the impassive Silence; she has found her fire. I hear of her as the charm of a brilliant court, as the soul of a nation of intrigue. Of her beauty one does not speak, but her talent is called prodigious. What impels me to ask the idle question, If it were well to save her life for this? Undoubtedly she fills a station which, in that empire, must be the summit of a woman's ambition. Delphine's Liberty was not a principle, but a dissatisfaction. The Baroness Stahl is vehement, is Imperialist, is successful. While she lives, it is on the top of the wave; when she dies — ah! what business has Death in such a world?

As I said, I have never seen Delphine since her marriage. The beautiful statuesque girl occupies a niche into which the blazing and magnificent intrigante cannot crowd. I do not wish to be disillusioned. She has read me a riddle, — Delphine is my Sphinx.

VI

AS FOR MR. HAY — I once said the Antipodes were tributary to me, not thinking that I should ever become tributary to the Antipodes. But such is the case; since, partly through my instrumentality, that enterprising individual has been located in their vicinity, where diamonds are not to be had for the asking, and the greatest rogue is not a Baron.

www.ingramcontent.com/pod-product-compliance
Lightning Source LLC
Chambersburg PA
CBHW020918180626
46816CB00007BA/2467